HENRY

HENRY

⊙ FINDS ⋅ HIS ⊙

WORD

BY LINDSAY WARD

**DIAL BOOKS
FOR YOUNG READERS**

an imprint of Penguin Group (USA) LLC

For Tyler

Dial Books for Young Readers
Published by the Penguin Group
Penguin Group (USA) LLC
375 Hudson Street
New York, New York 10014

USA / Canada / UK / Ireland / Australia / New Zealand / India / South Africa / China
penguin.com
A Penguin Random House Company

Library of Congress Cataloging-in-Publication Data

Ward, Lindsay, author.
Henry finds his word / by Lindsay Ward.   pages cm
Summary: Baby Henry is ready to talk, but first he must search for the perfect first word.
199-9303   ISBN 978-0-8037-3990-1 (hardcover)
1. Infants—Juvenile fiction. 2. Speech—Juvenile fiction. [1. Babies—Fiction.
2. Speech—Fiction.] I. Title.
PZ7.W214316He 2014   [E]—dc23   2013035183
Manufactured in China on acid-free paper
1 3 5 7 9 10 8 6 4 2

Designed by Mina Chung • Text set in Hockey is Life
This art was created using pencil and pastel.

Henry was looking for a word.
His first word.

It was all his mama and papa talked about.
They were so excited.

What do you think he'll say?

When will he say it?

Henry didn't know what the big deal was.
He said lots of stuff all the time.

"RAH RAH RAH RAH RAH!"

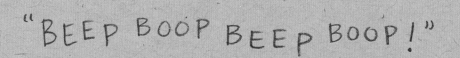

"BEEP BOOP BEEP BOOP!"

"WOO WOO woo WOO WOO WOO woo WOO."

Henry thought he was perfectly clear about what he wanted. But it took his mama forever to figure out that "bbbghsh" meant "bottle."

Or "no!"

Or "book."

Or "ball."

So Henry decided to try and find his word.

It would help if he knew what to look for.
But Henry wasn't sure what words looked like.

Were they **small**?

BIG?

FUZZY?

PRICKLY?

L O N G ?

SHORT?

Henry searched everywhere.

He checked under his blankie.

He looked in his crib.

He dumped out his toy box.

No words.
Not a single one.

"Harrumphhh!"

So Henry decided to ask
some of his friends for help.

He asked Cat if he
knew any words.

He asked Bird.

CHIRP
CHIRP
CHIRP
CHIRP
CHIRP

Nope, that didn't sound right either.

He asked Bunny.

But Bunny just sniffed him
and hopped away.

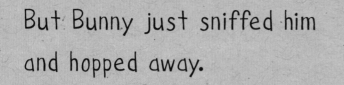

Henry looked up for his mama.
But she was nowhere in sight.

Henry began to cry.

Where was she?

He needed her!

Henry cried and cried, louder and louder.
Then the hiccups came. Henry *hated* hiccups.

And then it happened. Deep down. Henry could feel it
rumbling inside him, ready to come out . . .

"Don't worry, Henry. I'm right here."

"Wait! Did you say Mama?"

Henry looked at her and smiled.

"Mama." Yeah, that sounded right.

MAMA!

MAMA!

MAMA!

Henry had finally found his word.
And he wasn't afraid to use it.

MAMA!

MAMA!

MAMA!

MAMA!

MAMA!

MAMA!

MAMA!

MAMA!

MAMA!

MAMA!

MAMA!

MAMA!

MAMA!

MAMA!

MAMA!

MAMA!

MAMA!

MAMA!

MAMA!

MAMA!

MAMA!

MAMA!

MAMA!

MAMA!

MAMA!

MAMA!